TAWANDA'S QUEST

A Novel

by

Brooke A. Burks, Ph.D.

A DocuBrooke, LLC Publication

Published by
DocuBrooke, LLC
Post Office Box 2652
Auburn, AL 36831

Follow us on Twitter @DocuBrooke
and Facebook: www.facebook.com/DocuBrooke
www.docubrooke.weebly.com

Cover Design & Layout by
DocuBrooke, LLC

Ebook formatted in the United States by
DocuBrooke, LLC

PUBLISHER'S NOTE

for
Branden, Jason, and Lauryn

"For I know the thoughts that I think toward you, saith the Lord, thoughts of peace, and not of evil, to give you an expected end"

--Jeremiah 29:11

Table of Contents

Foreword

The novel you are about to read is about the life of a girl who is trying to cope with her brother's death. Unfortunately, this is a reality for so many young people today. We watch television reports or read news articles every day that speak of violence amongst teenagers. The story we never see, however, is how the people these teenagers leave behind are affected. They have mothers, fathers, sisters, brothers, cousins, aunts, uncles whom they leave to grieve the loss of such a young life.

For years now, the notion of I'm-gonna-get-mine-if-it-means-taking-yours has been rampant in the Black community. When will we wake up? When will we see that killing someone over a few dollars or a pair of shoes or a girl or a boy or a color is not the answer? We need to blame the parents. But, many parents teach their children to be good citizens. Oh, it's the media. But, the media does report the things that actually happen. So, are they lying? Oh, it's the teachers. But, the teacher's job is to teach content.

At the end of the day, parents must work harder, the media must not only report the damaging news, teachers must demonstrate care and concern, and everyone must work for the good of all children. We all have a responsibility to teach.

So let's teach love. I know it's hard sometimes to love some people. I see them on my job all the time. They come in early in the morning already looking as though they've had a bad day. Then they grumble, mumble, and complain for the rest of the day. People like that can be difficult to love, yet we must. It's the only way to survive and be happy with ourselves.

I know this has all been said before. Maybe this time, though, someone will get the message. If not through what I've written here, then through Tawanda's story. I have known this young lady for quite some time, and her story teaches love in a remarkable way. Enjoy.

Dr. Angela Trishelle Vantage Turnbaum

June 2001

Prologue:

A Situation That Caused Me to Change

Mrs. Carson's Fourth Grade English Class

1992

Last summer my big brother Marcus was killed by a gunshot to the heart on the corner of 52nd and Boston Avenue in Newark, where we live. I didn't stop eating like crazy people on T.V. who whine about needing to lose five more pounds as if the problem is gonna sweat away with the fat. I didn't start smoking like people who think that a puff is going to clear their minds and ease their troubles. And, I didn't start drinking like people who think that somebody wrote the answer to their problem on a post-it-note and stuck it to the bottom of a bottle. Instead, I started writing.

Folks on our stick-your-nose-in-other-folks-business side of town are always wondering what a nine-year-old could really have to write about. I got lots. My big brother Marcus was the type of person who would knock you down and fan you with a brick, as my grandma would say, if you messed with his little sister. He was always taking up for me when simple-Sarah-wanna-be-a-flower would start her mess about me being round as a Halloween pumpkin. I'd tell her she was just as ugly as one, and then Marcus would step in. In the first place, I wasn't round at all – she was just doing that "projection" stuff the shrink told me about: putting off on me the thing she really didn't like about herself. That was definitely Sarah. She was always pretending to be the best at most things when it was quite obvious to the rest of us that she was a fluke at everything. During the spelling bee in first grade, she just knew she was gonna win when she got the word "bait." You have to understand the sheer coincidence here. We had argued over the spelling of this word just the day before. Sarah said, "T-wanda, you know it's spelt b-a-t-e like *ate* with a *b* on the front." I told her that was nonsense just like those ridiculous turquoise jelly sandals she had on with her red and white polka dot one-piece short set. I tried to convince her of the b-a-i-t spelling, but she wouldn't hear of it. Imagine her surprise when she lost. At least I got Honorable Mention.

So, when me and Marcus were walking up 52nd at 2:17 on a Wednesday afternoon last July and Harold and his gang shot my brother and didn't even try to run 'cause they wanted me to know it was them who'd done it, I started writing. My mama says I must be half out my mind to start this writing stuff. I sit there on the third pew on Sunday mornings at Ecclesiastical Baptist Ministries, while Pastor Clemmings is screaming about some people supposed to be following Jesus, and I just write on the back of the "Sermon Notes" section of the program. This drives my mama up the wall and I can always tell she's mad at me when I do this 'cause she's sitting in the choir stand with her lips pursed like she just ate a lemon. My daddy doesn't even like taking me to the store with him 'cause I nearly ran into the stack of Charmin tissue one time trying to write.

Mama sent me to this doctor lady to see if something was wrong in my head. She made me look at all kinds of stupid stuff she called pictures. Looked like somebody just got tired of trying to paint a masterpiece and just threw the rest of the paint on the paper. Then, the lady wants me to tell her what it is. And I'm the one supposed to be crazy? In my own defense, I say writing helps me keep my memories of Marcus 'cause I write about him all the time and I don't wanna forget. Everybody got their opinions about how I need to be thinking about my future now.

Sister Calkins stared at me the whole service last Sunday. For a minute I thought maybe she had a glass eye that just wouldn't move when she turned her head. Then she came up to me after church and said, "Baby, you doin' okay? Ya mama tol' me you startin' to write a lot. You eatin' good?" I don't try to make nobody understand me. I'm just a kid. I told my mama about her staring at me during church, and whatduya know, she does have a glass eye.

People like Suzy Kerkowitz wanted to make everybody think she had her whole life laid out on a map and that she doesn't have a thing to worry about when she graduates from Oak Grove Magnet High School (for those supposed to be real smart folks) and goes to Yale University and then to some lawyer school across the globe in Washington, D.C. She said she couldn't help it if her parents could afford the finer things in life. That's what she used to say last summer before her daddy got laid off from the Nissan plant and left her mama and them five kids to take care of their own selves. Now, Suzy ain't got much to say about nothing.

So, I don't go around making people think I'm all that 'cause I write. I don't show anybody my work 'cause it's personal. Me and Marcus did so much he'd be mad if I told everybody about that time we skipped school and went to Auntie Cicily's Chicken Shack and set the big chicken in front of the store on fire. (Nobody ever knew it was us, so that's just between me and you.) So, I don't know if I ever will write a book about it. I don't even really know why Marcus got shot. I knew Harold and his boys didn't like him, but so what? I don't like lil' miss primp and curl Laura, but I ain't killed her yet. I just laugh at folks like that.

So, Marcus getting shot was the situation that changed me. Now, I'm a writer. When I grow up, I'm going to be the best book writer New Jersey has ever seen. Nobody believes me right now. Everybody's too busy worrying 'bout how I'm holding up since Marcus died. They don't have much to worry about. Marcus told me to never stop being Tawanda Michelle Billups no matter what, and I am sticking to my promise.

2007

"Tawanda, are you going to cook anything? We're starving." My mama knows I don't cook, so I don't know why she's asking this question. It's not that I can't cook. I think I do okay, but I just don't enjoy it. I know what's coming next.

"You know you won't find a husband without being able to cook." She side-eyes me and grins, knowing that I hate when she says that.

I've been out of college a whole year, getting my career going. "Who has time for a man, Mama?" I ask. My little sister, Shanice, thinks it's hilarious. "Even I have a boyfriend, T," she says.

I roll my eyes at Shanice. "Good for you. I, however, have better things on my agenda. You should be worrying about graduating high school, young lady."

"Oh, you definitely don't have to worry about that," she says, rolling her little neck. Shanice has always been petite and attitudinal. It's really cute though. "I make straight A's and so does Corey."

I wave her off with my hand and tell my mama that I've ordered food for us. "Is this what y'all do in D.C.? Order food every day? I guess you just don't know what to do with all that civil engineering money, huh?" Mama asks. We all laugh knowing that the big bucks haven't quite started rolling in yet.

"You know what?" Mama begins. "Remember those stories you used to write when you were in elementary and middle school? Why don't you put them into a book? I know there are some other young people out there who could benefit from them. I can't say that I would really enjoy reading them since I know they're all about Marcus, but I think it would be a good thing."

I paused for a moment, fondly remembering my big brother Marcus. All of my stories surround him as he was the highlight of my life. He would've been right here with us laughing at my desire not to cook. Whenever anyone mentions anything about him, my heartstrings pull ever so gently.

Shanice chimes in, "Yeah, T. You only let me read like one of 'em. Let me see what all the hype was about your writing."

Maybe they're right. Maybe my stories can help somebody. Shanice didn't real y get to know Marcus, so the stories could help her to learn who he was to me.

"Mama, Shanice," I start, "I think you're right. I guess when you go back home you can tell everybody I said that."

Miss Vantage

1994

I really stopped caring about school when my brother Marcus died three years ago. All I wanted to do was write about him. I went from straight A's to straight D's. Just doing enough to pass. That was until I met my sixth-grade English teacher, Miss Vantage.

Miss Vantage was the meanest teacher you ever wanted to meet. All of us kids hated her. I remember when Marcus was in her class. He used to plot out ways to get back at her for making him write essays on stupid stuff like the importance of breakfast. I figured Miss Vantage had better watch out 'cause Marcus was known to pull a fast one on you in his day. One time he tricked Mr. McCorvey, the sixth-grade science teacher, into believing that Marcus had thrown up all over the assistant principal Ms. Delasky and that she told everyone to go home early. After a while, Marcus stopped complaining about Miss Vantage and started doing his homework.

I guess Mama must've gotten on to him about his grades.

Anyway, Miss Vantage would come in every day with her granny dress and pink sweater she kept hanging on the back of her chair for those chilly mornings and peek over the top of her glasses to see if we were cheating on a test or talking or any of the many things us kids do like sneak in our book bags and eat potato chips and Skittles. Every week, Miss Vantage had the same boring routine. Every Monday was a quiz on something she knew nobody was gonna read over the weekend. Every Tuesday was a spelling test on words like "misconstrue." I mean, the lady thought we were supposed to be geniuses. I would use some of her words sometimes just so she'd know that I was not dumb. So, she pushes her horn-rimmed toad glasses back on her face and tells us one Wednesday 'bout this big test we were gonna take at the end of year. I was glad she finally mentioned something was gonna end. Seemed like she was the Energizer Bunny 'cause she never stopped going.

Now, don't get me wrong. When I want to do my work, I do my work. It's just that Miss Vantage couldn't figure out when that was. Like yesterday. She come givin' us some notes on William Shakespeare like he's somebody we really need to know about. He ain't shaking nothing up over here on A Street, so he can go on back to England or wherever it is he come from.

Anyway, she comes talking about this big test. "Tawanda, dear, you're going to fail my class if you don't start studying for this big test," she'd say. Like I'm the only one not studying. Everybody else ain't studying either. My mama told me to just let stuff like that go, so I did. Miss Vantage ain't worth getting' no butt-whippin' over. The doctor lady my mama used to make me visit right after Marcus died would tell me stuff about how to "cope with anger." She said that I should take deep breaths in and deep breaths out. If you ask me, that just takes up too much time. I'd much rather prefer to beat you down and breathe later. But, I knew I couldn't do that to Miss Vantage 'cause like I said, she ain't worth no whippin'.

So, I go home and start my math just before my mama gets home 'cause that's my favorite subject. My little sister Shanice likes to make Mama think she doing her work and gettin' good grades. Of course, if you're in kindergarten, everybody makes S's. Big deal.

"T-baby, you studying for that test Miss Vantage givin' y'all at the end of the semester?" Mama asks. Now, I'm wondering just how she knows about this big test.

"Yes ma'am."

"Don't look like it to me. Look like you doing math. You doing okay in that class. I want to see you study for that big test Miss Vantage givin'."

I am so mad. Miss Vantage done called my mama on her job and told her about a test. Ain't that something? I always knew she didn't have a life, but you just don't stop my mama from welding pipes together with a blow torch to tell her 'bout her child ain't doing something in school. She even called

21

Mama about Marcus one time. She said Marcus is "just not performing as well as he can. He has so much potential. He wrote an essay that I just loved. I always knew he had it in him. I just wish he'd continue on this path." Blah, blah, blah. She didn't know Marcus, and she doesn't know me. I'm sure she probably told Mama the same thing about me this time. I could just kill Miss Vantage sometimes.

Anyway, this big test finally comes up on a Friday – our last day in her class (Praise God!). She says all her usual stuff at the beginning of every test: Don't cheat; Don't look like you 'bout to cheat; Don't avert your eyes; Don't help nobody else cheat. I'm ready for this 'cause, like I said, my mama made sure I was studying for this crazy lady's test. Then, she goes to passing them out. When I get mine, it got a note on it from Miss Vampire herself. I figure she's trying to be funny 'cause I sneak a peek at the girl next to me and hers don't have no note on it.

When I open the note, it says:

Tawanda Billups,

I have thoroughly enjoyed having you in my class this semester. Although I know you could have easily earned an A in my class, you chose the easy route and did only what was necessary to pass. After our first encounter in class, you promised you would do at least half of what Marcus did in class. Well, I commend you. You did what you said you would do and got exactly what you wanted. I wonder what your brother Marcus would think about this. Would he be proud?

Sincerely,

Miss Annie T. Vantage

I felt the red-hot blood bubbling over in my veins. I wanted to get up and choke her right then. How dare she put Marcus in this? He's *my* brother. *I'm* the one he loved and protected. *I'm* the one who bought him his favorite shirt for Christmas one year, and he bought me my favorite bracelet. *I'm* the one who he encouraged to do the best. She doesn't know him. *I'm* the one who stood as Harold's bullet went into my brother's heart. *I* was the one there holding him as he bled to death, screaming in pain while it took hours for the ambulance to get there. *I* was the one who comforted him during his last minutes, making sure he died in peace. *I* was only in the third grade, but I was a big girl and did what I could for my big brother. *I* was the one who heard his last words: "I love you, T-baby. Always remember that you are beautiful and that you can do whatever you want."

Tears now streamed down my face. The first time I've cried for Marcus since his funeral. All of my memories of Marcus came into my head at one moment: the time we burned down the big chicken in front of Aunt Cicily's Chicken Shack; the time we sneaked into the movies to see an R-rated film; the time we went to Panama City Beach with Daddy to go swimming in the big waves.

I knew I had to get myself together. After all, I *am* Tawanda Billups, and I *do* have a reputation to uphold. So, I turned my test over and read the two questions on the paper.

1. Write three paragraphs about how your experience in this class this semester has benefited you.

or

2. Do an oral report (impromptu) on how your experience in this class this semester has benefited you.

Everybody knows I'm a natural-born writer, but I glanced around the room and saw everybody taking option number one. I, of course, must dare to be different, so I took the number two option. I raised my hand to be noticed by the old sewer rat, and she told me to stand before the class and give my report. I had no idea of what to say. I was so mad at Miss Vantage, I couldn't even think straight. It felt like I had been standing there for two hours before I even opened my mouth. Then, I thought of something Marcus once told me: "Never look like you're afraid to do anything 'cause then people will think you're a wimp and take advantage of you."

"We're waiting," the old prune said.

"Well," I started, "I came to this class with the preconceived notion that Miss Vantage was an evil little woman who treated students like crap because she was trying to get back at a teacher who did her like that sixty-five years ago. In some ways, I can see the truth behind that notion. However, this class has helped me learn words like 'meander' and 'agitation.' For that, I am eternally grateful." I looked directly at Miss Vantage and even though I was saying such mean things about her, she looked at me with sadness in her eyes. I thought she would stop me right there and send me to the principal's office, but she didn't. I looked back at my classmates who looked shocked that I had called Miss Vantage evil.

Suddenly, I didn't feel so good about the things I'd said. My palms started to sweat, and I licked my lips. I looked back at Miss Vantage who gestured for me to continue. I looked down at my hands and said,

"My brother Marcus would be very proud of me because I am standing up for what I believe in... But he wouldn't be proud of the fact that I just skated by in your class. Even though he wasn't an A-B student, he knew that I was. Since he died, I've really stopped caring – until now. No, Marcus wouldn't be proud of that. As he was dying, he told me that I was beautiful and that I could do whatever I want to. I thought that meant I could cut up if I wanted to or fail if I wanted to. But now I know what he was saying. I can be whatever I want to be. If I do well in school and go to college, I can really be somebody besides the Tawanda who lives on A Street. So, Miss Vantage, I apologize. Not for keeping my word. But I apologize for just doing enough to get by."

I couldn't believe those words had just come out of my mouth. Even Be-Bop McGhee, the twin I beat up last year for talking about my brother when he knew Marcus has whupped his behind plenty of times before, was surprised. I guess I had learned something after all. Who would have ever thought?

27

When I went to my seat, Miss Vantage looked at me with tears in her eyes and said, "Tawanda, we all miss Marcus. He was a wonderful student. Yes, he got into some trouble every now and then, but he was an excellent writer, just like you. You may not believe this, Tawanda, but Marcus wrote his best essay about you. He adored you and loved you to death. There's nothing that he wouldn't have done for you."

I reached into my book bag, which had my whole life in it, and pulled out the little wooden jewelry box that Marcus had made in wood shop class one year. I have lots of Marcus's things. I walked up to Miss Vantage and gave her the box.

"Marcus made this for me, and I want you to have it."

"Why?" she asked.

"I have everything of Marcus's. And, I have memories that no one else does. I see now that you loved him, too. So, here's something for you to remember him by."

Miss Vantage is my favorite teacher.

Mr. Havisham

(1989)

About five years ago when Marcus was living and I was six and Shanice was just being born, Marcus and I got into so much trouble, the folks at church with their love-to-gossip-and-talk-about-other-folk-children selves thought for sure we'd end up in the pen or in the ground. For one of us, they were right, but I don't like to be a supporter of their two-faced correctness, so I won't. It's not Marcus's fault he got shot.

Anyway, the one thing I remember us getting in the most trouble for, which wasn't the time we burned up the big chicken in front of Aunt Cicily's Chicken Shack by the way, was the time Marcus and I flooded Mr. Havisham's meat market. We didn't do it on purpose. It sort of just happened ...

"T, let's go get some garlic bologna from Mr. Havisham's," Marcus said.

"Okay." I never denied a request from Marcus even if I didn't really feel like it. He knew I just

29

enjoyed being with him, so it didn't matter where we went or what we did.

Mr. Havisham's store was no more than five and a half blocks up from where we lived on A Street. I knew we shouldn't have gone when Mama said, "Don't get into any trouble, you two." I knew she had jinxed us then.

Of course, on our way, we had to pass by the Jones clan who never stayed in the house but always wanted to be outside in other people's business. Their mother had the odd quirk of naming each of her children after a month of the year. This particular day, only September Jones was outside.

"Where *y'all* going?" she asked in that I-need-to-know-on-pain-of-death tone.

"To mind our business." Marcus rolled his eyes, and I knew then that he was already aggravated with September. She never knew when to stop.

By that time, Mrs. Jones came wobbling down the front steps no doubt eagerly awaiting the twelfth, and hopefully last, of the Jones crew.

"Hi, Mrs. Jones," I waved. "When is December due?"

"Hi there, Tawanda. I haven't decided to name her December just yet. What do you think about 'Melanie'?"

Why on America's soil would she all of a quickness decide to not name a baby after a month? "Sounds great," I lied. Marcus and I giggled and ran the rest of the way to Mr. Havisham's. I figured this garlic bologna better be worth it today.

Now, there's something you should know about Mr. Havisham. Even though he's the nicest man in our neighborhood, he won't let you leave his store without washing your hands. Big Money Sid told us once that Mr. Havisham did that because one of his daughters got food poisoning after not washing her hands before she ate.

"You know little Barishka, man, she ate some food and didn't wash her hands and then the next thing you know she was in Grace and Mercy (the Hospital) gettin' some serious attention from Dr. Pate 'nem and she almos' died for real like that." Big Money Sid talked in long, elaborate sentences. None of us liked talking to him because we never knew when the sentence would end. He was like a five-year-old who hooks all his sentences together with "and." He was, however, the source of a lot of information. When we wanted to know who stabbed Willie Joe Nelms, Big Money Sid got phone calls all day long. When Mrs. Blankenship, who swore she was fifty but was obviously near eighty, was suspected to be "courting" (as the old folks say) a younger man, it was Big Money Sid who found out it was Willie Joe Nelms and that was why he got stabbed (by Mr. Blankenship).

We had no reason to doubt Big Money Sid. After all, he was in the streets more than anybody else, and he loved hanging around Mr. Havisham's store for whatever reason. He had even been accused of being a peeping Tom, so we knew at least some of his stories had to be true.

So it made sense that Mr. Havisham had us wash our hands before we left his store each time. When Marcus and I walked in, Mr. Havisham greeted us with his usual formality.

"Hi, kids. What can I do you for today?"

"We just want some garlic bologna," Marcus said. "About a pound."

"Coming right up." Mr. Havisham pulled out the tube of bologna and began slicing it on his machine. I watched as the heavy steal glided smoothly back and forward, back and forward, cutting each piece into thin round shreds. "How's your mom?" he asked.

"She's great," Marcus replied. He looked at me as I stared at the back and forward motion of the meat cutter. Then he bumped my arm. "Stop it," he whispered.

"What?" Did I do something wrong?

"Stop staring at the thing. You look crazy doing that."

"Sorry, geez."

"There you go, kiddos. One pound. And don't forget to go around the side here and wash your hands." Mr. Havisham smiled and handed Marcus the brown paper bag. "This one's on the house," he said.

"Thanks," I started.

"No, that's okay, Mr. Havisham. We'll pay for it," Marcus said reaching into his pants pocket for the money.

"Look," Mr. Havisham began, "you kids come in here all the time. The least I can do is give you this one free. You're good customers and good kids."

"Thanks, but no thanks," Marcus said. "We don't take no handouts."

I was a bit disappointed since we could've had it for free, but I guessed Marcus must have had a reason behind it. I was sure he would tell me later.

We walked around the side to wash our hands, when Marcus dropped the paper bag into the sink.

At first we thought nothing of it. A paper bag falls into a sink – you get it out. Easier said than done, though. Mr. Havisham's sink was one of those big industrial ones you see in places like the hotel kitchen where my daddy worked on weekends or the kind you see in high school cafeterias like the one at Oak Grove Elementary. Any other time, Mr. Havisham's old green paint bucket would be sitting out for us to stand on. Not today. Neither Marcus nor I had arms long enough to reach down to the drain.

I cupped my hands, ready for Marcus to step into them and reach into the sink, but there was no way I could hold his weight. Then we tried him cupping his hands for me to step in, but I was still too short to reach the bag in the drain. It would have made all the sense in the world to just call Mr. Havisham, but we don't always see things when we should, and hindsight, as they say, is 20/20.

Now Marcus is always one to come up with a bright idea when we're in trouble. This time, he suggested that if we turn the water on, the bag would float out of the drain, and then we could reach it. Some bright idea.

35

Marcus struggled to reach and turn the water on, which he finally accomplished after a minute or two. As the sink began to fill up, we noticed that the bag wasn't moving. Instead, it had lodged itself in the drain and refused to come out.

"What are we going to do, Marcus?" I cried. Sweat beads now took residence on my forehead. I felt sick all over. Marcus, as usual, put on that I'm-cool-nothing-can-bother-me look, but I could tell he was just as scared as I was.

"We're going to turn the water off and fish out the bag," he replied while attempting to turn the water off. For some reason, he couldn't grip the faucet handle like the first time. Instead of pushing back on the handle, Marcus pushed forward and more water gushed out.

I ran around the corner to the counter where Mr. Havisham had been standing, but he was no longer there. "Mr. Havisham," I called. No answer. "Mr. Havishaaaaam." He must have gone out the back to his office. I was on my way to get him when

Marcus called, "Tawanda!" It was one of those squeaky, voice-changing yells that started out in a low "Ta" and ended in a high "wanda."

As I headed back to the sink where Marcus was, I could see water gliding across the floor. Marcus was still standing at the sink trying to turn it off. But more and more water poured onto the floor as I scrambled to get the low-lying paper bags of flour, meal, and sugar. I looked into Marcus's eyes for some sign of hope, but to no avail. What I saw was terror, remorse, and shame.

Just as the water was nearing Mr. Havisham's barrels – he kept flour and sugar in these for people who wanted to buy it by the cupful – Marcus yelled, "I got it T! I got it!" By that time, I was scrambling around all over the store picking up things off the floor. I didn't hear the water running anymore. I ran around to the sink, and Marcus was standing there grinning with every stitch of his clothes drenched.

"What's going on in here?" That was Mr. Havisham, finally making it into the store from

37

wherever it was he'd been. I thought Wow, what a great time to show up. We could've used you about two minutes ago.

Marcus began, "Mr. Havisham, we're really sorry. We were trying to wash our hands and we couldn't get the water back off."

"Yeah," I chimed in, "we called for you, but we didn't know where you were. We're really sorry."

"We'll work for you every evening to make up for whatever we damaged, sir," Marcus said, and I wanted to know just who he thought he was to volunteer my services without my consent. But, I knew he was right. Either that or face the wrath of Mama, which we were definitely going to do anyway.

"I see you tried to get most of my flour and sugar out of the way." Mr. Havisham took a quick survey of his store and decided it wasn't so bad. "Far as I can tell, only two bags of flour got messed up. I'll let you off the hook this time, but please remember to use the stool okay?"

"Yes, sir," Marcus and I said in unison. I started to tell him that the stool wasn't there or we would've used it, but Marcus hit me in the side – his way of saying "Shut up, let's go."

"You think he's gonna tell Mama?" I asked as Marcus and I walked back up A Street towards our house.

"Naw, Mr. Havisham is cool peeps. But, Mama's gonna want to know how our clothes got so wet."

"Should we lie?'

"Just follow my lead."

I completely trusted him. "Hey, why do you think Mr. Havisham wanted to give us the bologna for free today? He's never done that before. I would've taken it."

"Look, just because somebody offers you something for free doesn't mean you have to take it. We have more pride than that." Marcus paused for a moment. He looked a little sad. "Mr. Havisham was gonna give us that bologna because we really don't

39

have the money right now, T. I'm not supposed to be telling you this, so keep your big mouth shut, okay?"

"But Mama and Daddy have jobs. They make good money, don't they?"

"Well, Daddy got laid off. That's just a nice way of firing you when they don't have enough money to pay you with. So, don't go asking for stuff you know they don't have the money for."

"I won't." I was a little sad, and then I was sorry. Two days ago I asked Mama for a Rainbow Brite doll. When she told me no, I pouted all the way home. I wish I hadn't done that.

We passed by the Joneses' house again, and just about everybody was outside. The two oldest boys were shooting craps on the side, April was braiding June's hair on the front porch steps, and July was sitting in the rocking chair sipping on lemonade. We tried to scoot by unnoticed, but October Jones came running up to us. She grabbed my hand and said, "Tawanna, you wanna play wif us? We got a dog. Her name Monday."

"No, me and Marcus gotta go home. Maybe next time."

By the time we got home, Mama was already at the door ready to grill us.

"Uh, huh, you soaking wet. I already know about it, so don't come telling me no lies. Who told you to go down to Havisham store? Y'all always running off down these streets. I keep telling y'all to stay in the yard and you won't get in no trouble. But, no, you gotta go down there and mess up that man's store. Get in here, now! Get out of those wet clothes and get ready for your whippin'!"

That was the last time Marcus and I got a whipping. We made a pact that we would not do any more crazy stuff that Mama might find out about, even though flooding Mr. Havisham's store wasn't really our fault. I still wondered how Mama found out about it. I know Mr. Havisham didn't tell her.

Then, I remembered – Big Money Sid.

Leaving Daddy

1995

My parents finalized their divorce last spring, and it was like all H-E- double hockey sticks broke loose. We moved to a no-name town in Alabama, and even though I didn't consider any of those two-faced snobs to be my friends, I was still going to miss the daily gossip, the smoggy morning breeze of Newark, New Jersey, and the greasy lunches at Oak Grove Middle School. Not that I have anything against the paper mill smells of Alabama, I just didn't want to live there. I would be closer to Grandma and Grandpa who had been desperately trying to get us to move down south since before Marcus died, though. Now, it was inevitable that we move. Daddy insisted on keeping the house, the cars, and even our little puppy Benji. "Why can't we at least take Benji?" I'd asked him.

"Because I bought him!" he yelled. "My money, my dog."

"Okay, okay," I said trying to calm him before he went on one of his yelling sprees.

"Get out of my way," he said pushing me into the wall while he reached for a beer in the refrigerator. This was an everyday routine. Going to the fridge to get a beer and plopping down on the already dilapidated couch in front of the TV with the remote in his right hand and his left hand down his pants. He sort of reminded me of a black Al Bundy on *Married with Children*.

"Tawanda, hit that light on," he mumbled. I immediately complied for fear that he would knock me over the head with his beer bottle. He probably wouldn't, though, seeing it was still half full.

"Daddy," I whispered, not wanting to pull his eyes away from the *What's Happening?* rerun on television. "Daddy," I whispered again easing up to the couch and sitting next to him. Should I lay my head on his shoulder? Should I put my arms around him? "Daddy."

"What?! Why do you keep calling me? Can't you see I'm watching T.V.?"

"Yes, but –"

"But nothing. Go outside and play or do something. Better yet, why don't you go on and pack your stuff, so you won't be waiting until the last minute."

"But, Daddy," I cried. I couldn't believe my ears. My Daddy who used to take me and Marcus fishing and to the beach and who used to love us. I was not going to take it any more.

"Suck it up, Tawanda," he said. "No crying around here. Take it like a man."

"That's just it, Daddy. I'm not a man. I'm not Marcus. He's dead, remember?" My entire face was wet by now. God, please don't let Mama walk in right now, I thought. Daddy got up from the couch and walked over to me. If I backed down now, he'd win.

"What did you say little girl? I am your father. You do not talk to me any ki—"

"Some Daddy you are. You just go around beating up on people, trying to prove you're 'the man.' You used to not be like this. You used to love us. What happened to you? All you do is eat, sleep, drink, and fart. You hardly go to work, yet you talk about all the stuff you bought. You want me to be your daughter, but you keep treating me like a man. I AM TWELVE YEARS OLD!" I was screaming then. I didn't know what had gotten into me.

I thought he was going to reach over and choke me, but he didn't. He just grabbed his mangled mass of keys from the end table and walked out the door. I sat on the couch crying for what seemed like hours before Mama and Shanice got home.

"Hey, T-baby," Mama called from the kitchen. I tried to clear my face before she saw me. "Come help your sister and me put up these groceries."

"Yes, ma'am. Here I come," I said still groping to wipe my face of any evidence of crying. As I walked into the kitchen, Mama looked at me with one eyebrow up.

45

"I know my children, and I know something's wrong," Mama said. "Did Martin hurt you?"

I was quiet for a moment. I knew if I told her what happened, she would probably kill him. I did love my Daddy, but I knew Mama didn't stand for no mess when it came to her kids.

"Tawanda," Mama said. I could see her nose flaring and her chest rising and falling heavily. She had put one hand on her hip and had gripped the side of the kitchen counter. I knew she meant business.

"Please tell me what happened here today before I get real upset."

"We got into an argument," I said looking down.

"About what?" I told her everything. Mama was the type you couldn't hide *anything* from. "He better not have hit you," she said.

"He didn't," I replied, not completely lying. It was a push, not a hit.

"This is it. My child should not have to defend herself against her own daddy. We're leaving today.

Girls, go get started packing your things. If it's not important, then leave it."

I cried as I walked to my room. Shanice, on the other hand, didn't seem to mind at all. Since her room and mine were exactly across from each other, I watched her grabbing suitcases, pulling clothes, dolls, shoes, and more dolls out and stuffing them haphazardly into the suitcases.

I only had two suitcases and a book bag. How would I pack all my things and Marcus's? I began to cry even more with this revelation. I couldn't even see what I was grabbing, so I just stopped and lay across the bed sobbing into my Winnie-the-Pooh pillow.
I felt Mama's hand rub my back as she sat on the bed next to me.

"T-baby, I know you're hurt, and I know you don't really want to do this, but don't you think it'll be better to move? You know we really have to, right?"

"I don't have room for Marcus's stuff," I cried looking up at Mama's strained face. She began crying too and took my face in her hands.

"Don't you worry. You're gonna pack some and I'm gonna pack some and Shanice is gonna pack some. Then, we're gonna leave a couple of things for Daddy, 'cause he misses Marcus, too," she explained.

"I love you, Mama," I said as she bent over to kiss my forehead. She always had the right answers.

*****

We've been in Alabama for almost a year now. It's not as bad as I thought. I really like being able to see Grandma and Grandpa whenever I want instead of having to write letters all the time and you sort of get used to the paper mill smell after a while.

As for Daddy, I still love him and always will. It took us leaving for him to realize the pain he had caused us. He was calling almost every day when we first got here, but he's slacked off a bit lately. Every time he calls, I remind him that I love him and he reminds me that one day we'll be together again, me and him, fishing on the pier.

Peeco, Shang, and Boolie

1997

After Aunt Debbie was sent upstate to a padded four-wall cell at Lindincare Facility for setting old Miss Hattie's dress tail on fire, my cousins Peeco, Shang, and Boolie came to live with us. I wasn't one to fancy lil' kids running around all day messing things up, so this of course was not going to fly. However, I eventually came to like the little pet peeves.

My sister Shanice thought it was great. She finally had somebody to boss around and play Barbie with. She knew I was not the one. After all, I was in the ninth grade; I couldn't be caught playing with dolls. I couldn't understand why their father, whoever he was, couldn't take them. According to Aunt Debbie, he'd prefer to not be bothered with children. According to me, he needs to step up to the bowl and do right for a change.

When the big day came for them to move in, our next door neighbor D'Sota, went to pick them up. I wasn't too fond of her, either. But when it came to

49

getting a job done, D'Sota was always up to the challenge.

"Well, here you are, kids," D'Sota started. "Your new home."

Before I could say "Hello," Peeco, Shang, and Boolie were all over the place like they owned it. They flopped down on our brand new love seat, spilled grape juice on the carpet, and had Mama's new lamp leaning precariously to one side. I thought surely we would be homeless in less than two days.

"Hey, guys," I said to them, "don't you want to see your new rooms? Mama spent extra time making sure you'd be comfortable."

"Sure," Peeco said. The others silently agreed and we were off on a tour to the end of the hall where the boys would be sleeping in my old room and then to the right where Shanice and Boolie would bunk. I had decided to move into the study on the other side of the house so I would be far away from those demolition derbies.

"So, Tawanda," Shang started, "where's Auntie Brenda?"

"She's at work, but she'll be home any minute now."

"Do we have to call her Mama now?" Boolie asked.

"Of course not," I replied. "You still have a mother. She's just getting some help right now."

"Duh, stupid," Peeco said shoving his sister Boolie to the wall.

"Hey! What are you doing?" I yelled at Peeco. "If you're going to live here, you have to get along."

"Where else are we going to live?" Shang asked sarcastically.

"Yeah, where?" Boolie repeated.

"Do you guys always talk in order?" I asked. These kids were really freaking me out. They talked in the order of their birth. First Peeco, then Shang, then Boolie each time.

"What do you mean?" Peeco asked. I then looked at Shang because I knew he'd be the next to speak.

"Yeah, what do you mean?" Shang asked.

We spent the whole evening taking turns talking. It was driving me up the ceiling, and I had better things to do like go jump off a skyscraper.

Mama had them enrolled in school the next day, and they became instantly popular in their classes. In two weeks, Mama had been to each teacher at least five times for behavior problems. The last straw was when Shang's teacher Mrs. Harris called. Mama put her on speaker phone so I could hear what those bugaboos were up to now. Mrs. Harris asked, "Ms. Billups, is Shang's real name Shang?"

"Yes," Mama said bewildered.

"His name should be Shame. Today after lunch, this Shang character climbed to the top of the monkey bars, showed us his peetie weetie, and urinated on Marsha Dewitt's head."

"Oh my God!" Mama exclaimed.

"Ms. Billups, I'm sorry, but these children cannot attend this school any longer. Two weeks has been long enough. I thought you were a good parent, but apparently not."

That in itself was enough to get Mama fired up.

"First of all," Mama started, "they are not my children. Secondly, how can you tell me what I'm good at and what I'm not. All these kids need is a little love, a little attention, and a lot of discipline, which, if you had been giving, this situation would never have occurred. I've never seen a teacher who can't control her own class. He doesn't climb poles at home. Must be something you're not doing at that school." Mama hung the phone up in her face then. "Tawanda, baby I know you're in high school now and you have things you want to do and I'm not trying to steal your adolescent years away from you as I'm sure you're assuming, but we have to work together to solve this. I can't home school them. You're smart. Help me think of something.

My mind was drawing blanks, question marks, and a couple of clowns. I didn't know what to do with those crazy kids. They had always been more than a handful. Whenever we went to visit Aunt Debbie, which wasn't as often as Christmas comes, Peeco, Shang, and Boolie were usually home alone running around like chickens ready for the fryer.

However, there was one time about three years ago when they actually pretended to be civilized. We were still living in New Jersey but came down to visit Grandma and Grandpa. No one really wanted to go see Aunt Debbie, but Mama insisted. When Mama rang the doorbell, a five-year-old Peeco snatched open the door and ushered us in. Aunt Debbie, they reported, was out with some "friends." Who in their right mind would leave a five-year-old, four-year-old, and one-year-old at home alone? That's when we really knew something was wrong with Aunt Debbie.

The kids were in good shape, though. Peeco had somehow cooked hotdogs and the three of them were watching Barney. After three and a half hours (it was now 11:35 p.m.), Aunt Debbie finally straggled in and explained that she had been discussing deep issues with her friends. "What kind of deep issues?" I'd asked as Mama shot me a glare. "Oh, like fishing and swimming. Stuff like that," she replied.

I told you Aunt Debbie was crazy. Now, she's at Lindincare and we have no idea what to do with her kids.

"Have you thought of anything yet?" Mama asked. I could see the thinking wrinkles in her forehead getting thicker as she thought harder.

"Why don't we just threaten them?" Shanice chimed in, walking down the hall to us.

"Why would you want us to threaten your new friends?" I asked.

"'Cause they're getting on my nerves. Boolie bit off Ken's arm, Peeco put a big hole in my stuffed Tigger, and Shang wrote on my blanket with a crayon. Please do something, Mama."

"I got it!" I yelled. "They seem to be each other's best friend, so why don't we separate them? Put them in separate rooms, separate schools, separate meal times. The works!"

"That's a great idea, Tawanda!" Mama high-fived me, and she took off to the schools while I started rearranging rooms. Within two days, life was better. Peeco, Shang, and Boolie learned to cherish the little time they had together. They knew that if they misbehaved, they wouldn't be able to spend time together. It was awesome. I never knew it was possible to separate three people who live in the same house. We could actually have conversations in which they didn't speak in order.

"Tawanda, you got a minute?" Peeco was standing at my door looking like he was about to cry.

"Sure," I smiled. I had been working on my five-page paper, but I could spare a few minutes. "What's up?"

"You know we've been here for five months now. Do you think Mom's ever coming back?"

"Yes, I do, Peeco. Your mom is really sick right now, so we don't want to rush it, but I know she's coming back. You're really missing her aren't you?"

"Yeah." I motioned for him to sit on the bed with me and we talked for hours and really had fun.

"Can I ask you another question?" Peeco timidly asked.

"Yes."

"Well, you know how me and Shang and Boolie can't see each other except on weekends?"

"Yeah," I replied slowly. Was Peeco trying to pull a fast one on me?

"What's it like not to see your brother Marcus ever?"

I was honored. No one had really ever asked me how I felt about losing Marcus. Except that so-called shrink who advised me to draw pictures of my feelings. I'm not Picasso, I'm Tawanda.

"It hurts," I told him. "When I see the three of you playing together and respecting each other, it reminds me of Marcus and me. I really do miss him. I hope you guys never have to experience being apart forever. If you continue like this, you guys will be much better off when you're older."

"Yeah, I guess you're right," he mumbled looking down at his hands.

Peeco, Shang, and Boolie stayed with us for three more months. Their teachers had grown to love them, and we were all sad to see them leave to move in with their father. He had never known he had three kids. He had always popped in and out of town. But now, he's going to be a real father. I think he's going to be a good one, too. We'll still get to see them on the weekends since they only live in the next city. But it won't be the same.

I never thought I'd see the day when I would say I miss Peeco, Shang, and Boolie, but I really do.

Thankful Divorce

1999

Ever since my parents divorced when I was 12, I've tried to figure out some way to thank them for not ruining my life with unending arguments over which one of them can't seem to figure out how to keep water off the bathroom floor after taking a shower or who incessantly forgets to close the windows when the air conditioner's on. Sometimes I'd pretend it was me just to get some peace.

Think about it. Who'd want to put up with someone telling you that you sneeze incorrectly and then demonstrate how it should be done? So, I'm glad they're divorced.

My wannabe friend (wannabe in that she keeps coming to my house after I've told her to go home several times, but Mama makes me be nice) Lydia Chardae Alfreda-Jo Thomas who always talks as if she's in some fairytale said, "Tawanda, you shouldn't be glad about your parents' divorce. Look at how the three little pigs turned out."

Now you're probably wondering the same thing I was. What do three fat porkers have to do with me and my parents? But I was sure Lydia would tell me, and she did.

"Well, they had good lives until one day they decided to leave their poor mother in search for their fortunes. And you know what happened? They were tortured by a mean 'ol wolf. Thank God the last one got away."

Lydia was an idiot in my book – not because she was dumb or anything. But just because we were juniors in high school and she still read "once upon a time" stories and played with Barbie dolls. I for one do not have time for such childish nonsense, and I told her so.

"I can't believe you would say that to my face, Tawanda."

"Would you rather I say it behind your back or under my breath or in my head? That's something you would do. You know I much prefer to look the horse in the mouth and tell it what it already knows."

I decided Lydia would be no help to me in finding a way to thank my parents. Granted, they have been divorced for four years now and we did have to move to this no-man's land Alabama and my crazy cousins did have to live with us for a minute while attempting to ruin my life, but all that is worth it to not have to live with two people getting into each other's faces about *clean* dishes sitting in the dishwasher.

But when I think about it, maybe there's nothing to thank them for. They're the ones who didn't know how to "process" Marcus's death. They sent me to some screwed up shrink, but they never once stepped into that or any other office.

They let Marcus's death destroy what they had spent years building. This realization kindled my hatred for Harold, the guy who shot my brother, once again. I hated his jealousy of Marcus. I hated that he couldn't be bold enough to simply talk to Marcus like I would have. My family could have been so perfect had it not been for Harold's cowardice.

Then I remembered something my cousin Boolie once told me when she lived with us. She said, "When I'm mad at my brothers for something they did to me, I just find something to laugh about because I know we'll be friends again tomorrow." I knew I'd never be friends with Harold, but I couldn't think about that. Marcus is never coming back. So, I must focus on what's right now.

In a way, I wish Mama and Daddy were still together, but reality is what's real. My counselor said to deal with each day as it comes (such a novel idea – go figure). So, I probably will never actually thank my parents for divorcing, but I can show them that I care.

Lydia came over again today and I told her that I'd decided to let the whole thank-my-parents-for-getting-divorced thing go.

"I'm so glad, Tawanda. You know it would probably hurt their feelings anyway. Just think of Dorothy in *The Wizard of Oz*. She spent all that time traveling down the yellow brick road with a dog and a few friends. When she got to the end, she found that what she was looking for she already had."

Now that made sense. I guess Lydia wasn't such an idiot after all.

Mr. Elgin Howard Lewis the Third

2000

Three months ago, Mama got married again. Didn't she know she was ruining everyone's life? Life was perfect before Mr. Elgin Howard Lewis the Third came on the scene. Out of nowhere, he pops up one rainy day in June and says, "Tawanda, I love your mother, and I've asked her to marry me." Who does he think he is? If he's even considering moving Elgin IV, Rascal (what kind of name is that?), and Martina in here with me, then he can forget about it.

"Mama must be pregnant," I said sharply.

"What makes you say that, sweetheart?"

"Third of all, I'm not your sweetheart, second of all, you don't have the right to question me, and first of all, isn't that why people get married when there's no other logical explanation?"

I knew I had him then. He just threw up his hands and started to walk away. He paused, trying to think of a good comeback, but, alas, he couldn't as I knew he wouldn't be able to. Then, he turned around and walked out of the room.

People can really work my nerves like that time Glenna Marrisette tried to pretend that my brother Marcus was the father of her five-month-old baby. At that time, Marcus had been dead for three years. I just laughed at her and shut the door on her big lop-sided chest.

Mama says I can be a trip sometimes. If you ask me, I'm a trip all the time. There's nothing better than surprising your own self with crazy stuff you do. For example, had I known I was going to sing the Star Spangled Banner while sliding down the flag pole at school, I probably still would have done it, but I wouldn't have been surprised. Life should be spontaneous.

I bet Marcus wished he could have been more spontaneous. Then again, he really was. When he was in the fifth grade, he told his teacher Mrs. McMurphy that our house was on fire and that he had to run home right away. When she asked him how he knew that, he said, "'Cause I can smell my G.I. Joe's plastic melting." Yeah, he *was* spontaneous.

"Tawanda, what is this I hear you telling Elgin?" Mama asked.

"You mean Elgin Howard Lewis the Third?"

Mama stood with her hands on her hips ready to backhand me any minute I was sure. I knew I had to choose my words carefully.

"Well," I started, "if you are pregnant then just know that I have a life, too, and that I cannot be expected to miss the prom to take care of a wailing baby. You do want me to enjoy my last two years of high school, don't you?"

"This has nothing to do with you, Tawanda, and you know I don't play that getting-smart-attitude either, so you better stop bumping your gums so much before I bump my belt across your behind." She paused for a moment. I do want Mama to be happy, but why does she have to get married to do it? It's supposed to be me, Marcus, Mama, Daddy, and Shanice. Nothing's going the way I planned. Why can't we be like regular people's families? Why did Marcus have to get killed? Why did Daddy have to leave? It's just not fair. I wanted to scream, but I knew doing so wouldn't help.

"Why do you hate Elgin so much?" Mama started again. "All he's ever tried to do is love you."

"I don't need him to love me. I got a daddy."

"Where is he, Tawanda? Do you know? Because I sure don't. I know you love your father. Elgin isn't trying to take his place."

"Well, why is he always trying to take me to the beach and get me to try some new food he's concocted?"

"Can't you see he's just trying to get close to you? Look, we're getting married, T-baby. Can you at least pretend to be happy for us?"

"Will his three degenerates be moving in with us?" Mama rolled her eyes then and turned around and walked out. Who wants a crackhead, a pimp, and a prostitute living with them? Not I, said the cat.

"Hey Tawanda!" Shanice called, running in and jumping on my bed. Was this barge-into-Tawanda's-room day?

"Hey," I mournfully replied.

"What's wrong with you?" she asked scrunching up her little nose. For the first time, I realized that I never really knew Shanice. Of course, I've lived with her for all of her ten years now, but we've never really talked. She was only two years old when Marcus died, and since then, I've been too preoccupied with losing Marcus to really be a big sister to her.

"Shanice, do you like Mr. Lewis?"

"You mean Elgin? Yeah, he's cool. Yesterday, we went to the zoo and we saw a rhinoceros. We also fed the monkeys through a little hole. They wouldn't let the monkeys eat out of our hands, so we had to throw the food in."

"You wanted monkeys to eat from your hands?"

"Yeah, it's neat. At school, my teacher brought a chimp named Panzee, and we got to rub him and feed him and stuff. Now that was cool. You think Mama'll let us get a chimp?"

"I doubt it. But what do you think about Elgin?" I was curious. If she liked him so much, maybe there was something to it.

"You don't like him, do you?" she asked.

"Not really, but I don't really know why."

"Yeah, I was like that, too, at first."

"What made you change your mind?"

"Well," she began, "I know I was little when Marcus died, so I don't remember much. But what I do remember after that was how mean Daddy was to us and Mama. I don't know what he was like before, but I know what he was like after. I haven't heard Mama laugh so much in her life now that Elgin's in the picture. He's good to us, Tawanda. I know you and Daddy and Marcus had good times before, but I think the way a person treats you now makes you forget how they used to treat you."

69

Wow, Shanice was really smart for a little girl of ten and I told her so. I vowed to spend more time with her. And maybe she's right. Maybe I should get to know Elgin a little better. Yeah, a few things probably will change, but maybe they're for the better. Mama's right, too. I haven't seen my daddy in almost a year. I guess I just have to get used to Mr. Elgin Howard Lewis the Third.

*****

Now, Mama and Elgin have been married for three months. It did take some time to get close to Elgin because I felt like I'd be betraying my father. After going to the movies with him and Shanice and baking brownies, cheese cakes, and sweet potato pies with them, I couldn't help but to like him a little bit. And, believe it or not, Elgin IV, Rascal, and Martina did not move in with us (Hallelujah!). They decided to stay with their mother. So, it's all working out for the good. Except one thing. Mama's been really sick lately, and I can't remember any other time she was

this sick than when she was pregnant with Shanice.
Oh my God!

"Mamaaaaaaa!"

The Curriculum

1999

I was in no mood for Mrs. Pelonis's class today. I had to ride a musty bus this morning, I forgot to bring my lunch money, and two teachers had already given me a half-ton of homework to do tonight. All I wanted to do was read something I could relate to. Something other than *The Crucible* or *The Glass Menagerie* for a change, but she was not hearing it.

"Young lady, are you implying that these great works of literature are not beneficial to your growth as an individual? I, for one, believe and know that learning about the Salem witch trials can and will teach you values that you can carry with you always."

See, that's what I'm talking about. Listening to the answer nearly put me to sleep, and that's what I should aspire to become after reading these "great works"? I think not. I like to read, but if Mrs. Pelonis keeps this up, then I'll have yet another mis-educational experience like last year in Mr. Johnston's class.

Now, don't get me wrong, pretty much everybody loves Mr. Johnston, but algebra became too distracting with his continuous "What do you think?" questions. It was quite frivolous if you ask me. One time right in the middle of solving a polynomial for x, he says, "Guys, I want you to put yourself in the x's place. What does that feel like?"

Of course, we all looked at him with blank stares as we silently prayed to be released from his algebraic prison. He would swear to us that there was some hidden conspiracy theory behind the entire education system, and he called himself trying to save us from it. (By the way, that's supposed to be G-13 classified information, so you didn't hear it from me.) So now, I hate math. I can't even walk into a checkout line at Wal-Mart without getting chills while my items are being scanned. Addition, subtraction, it's all a nightmare.

Anyway, I told Mrs. Pelonis that I wanted to learn the stuff we "had to" learn, but I wanted to do some side reading, too. Of course, everybody else in the class got on my case about not wanting to do extra work, but I considered it fun to read something that didn't have to do with soliloquies and murder. However, I was still unable to convince Mrs. Pelonis that we needed a little flavor in the curriculum.

She replied, "Tawanda, if you want school to be 'fun,' then you should go visit Ms. Purifoy's class down the hall. They do whatever they want, but how many of them pass the Graduation Exam? How many of them become successful in life? None... Now, back to *The Scarlet Letter.*"

"But, Mrs. Pelonis -- "

"No time for discussion dear. Who can tell me just what Hester's problem was..."

No such luck with Mrs. Pelonis. I read something about people like her once. I think they call them rational humans or something like that.

I was glad to finally get to Mr. Little's Chemistry class. Not that I liked Chemistry all that much, but Mr. Little made it so easy to understand.

"Well, Tawanda, what seems to be the problem today?" He spoke in that Southern drawl that only he could get away with and make people love it.

"You don't wanna know, Mr. Little."

"Sure, I do. I can't begin to teach you until you get your problems off your chest."

So, I told him everything about my day down to last block with Mrs. Pelonis. Surprisingly, he listened. Everybody else, however, had decided to take a little siesta in the meantime. Kenneth, only my best friend in the whole wide world, was even lying on the floor, but Mr. Little didn't seem to mind.

"Thanks for listening, Mr. Little."

"No problemo, Tawanda. You're a good kid, and I'm sure you'll be fine. Class, listen up. I don't want any of you to leave this class without learning. If you learn what's explicitly outlined in my lesson plan, that's great. But if you learn a life lesson, somethin' you can tote with you forever, then that's even greater."

I agreed with Mr. Little. There was something about learning what wasn't in the intended curriculum that I found exciting. But honestly, I can even see Mrs. Pelonis's point. I know she'll never bend to letting us read an Eric Jerome Dickey novel or anything like *Sula* by Toni Morrison, but as long as I can sneak into my book bag every now and then and eat Starbursts or a chicken sandwich, then I think I can learn whatever there is to offer.

Hannah

1998

I don't too much fancy big houses. The one with the white picket fence in the cul-de-sac on Mandarin Drive belongs to Hannah Johnson. At least she thinks it's hers. She gets on my nerves with her wannabe-rich-but-only-fifteen-years-old-self. Her parents are extremely wealthy, but she's the only one flashing the Benjamins. Kids these days are a trip and a half.

Yeah, I'm the same age as Hannah, but I'm old enough to whip Hannah and her big sister's butt all up and down New Hampshire Avenue. I have been known to do it before, so I wouldn't push my luck.

Anyway, Hannah comes to school crying yesterday and claims she broke a nail. Yeah right. You don't get called over the PA system to report to the guidance office for a broken nail. Plus, you don't leave Mrs. McElroy's class for nothing, not even if your right arm is gushing blood. So, I knew it must be serious.

But I'm not nosy, so I wasn't gonna ask. But then she made me mad.

"What're you looking at, Tawanda?" she asked, in a very nasty attitude I might add, when she finally got back to class. By this time, we were in fourth block history with Mr. Hanks.

"Not much," I responded to her stupid question. In my opinion, that's how you react to folks like that. My mama always told me to call 'em like I see 'em and don't take no stuff from nobody.

"Very funny." Her eyes were really red, like she just finished her forty-second shot of moonshine. "I guess you'd like to know what's wrong with me."

"Not really. You look like a tractor trailer just hit you though."

"You don't have to be so cruel, Tawanda."

"'Cruel' is my middle name. Besides, I'm trying to get my work done. You do know what that is, don't you? Mr. Hanks won't be gettin' on my case today."

"That's just like you to be so uncaring. Of all people, you should be the one to show some compassion."

She really shouldn't have gone there. I knew she was referring to Marcus whom she didn't even know.

But, just like everyone else, she knew my brother meant everything to me. I couldn't believe she was trying to use my brother's death to get some sympathy. I could just lay her out on this raggedy brown carpet, but I don't have time for folks like Hannah. Besides, I'm trying to pass tenth grade. A fight right now wouldn't be helping me. I guess things really are a bit screwed up in their little red-brick-white-picket-fenced house.

"Tawanda and Hannah, quiet down and finish your work," Mr. Hanks chimed in. I knew fussing with Hannah was gonna get me in trouble.

"See!" I whispered.

"Tawanda, I was just–"

Just then the bell chimed, signaling the end of the day. Hallelujah!

"Oh, lookie there," I said. "The bell just rang. Gotta go catch my ride."

"Tawanda, don't leave just yet."

"Why are you so eager to talk to me today? Any other day you wouldn't give me a second glance. I didn't think you had time to take your nose out of the clouds long enough to see us little people down here. So what's the big deal today?" She looked like she wanted to cry then. I didn't know what was going on.

"I'm... I'm... I'm pregnant," she sighed.

"You're what?!"

"Preg—"

"Yeah, yeah, I heard you the first time. Hannah, how could you let this happen? Better yet, why are you telling me?"

"Well, even though you are like the tomboy of the school and you have very few friends, I thought you were level-headed, someone I could confide in."

I don't know why I didn't just run. Not only did I miss my ride, but I also subjected myself to her continuous insults.

"Ok, I guess I'm all ears," I said. "Who's the father?"

"That's really none of your business," she said. Then I got up to leave. "Josh Ramsey," she said.

"The football jock, huh? Too bad. Look, Hannah, I don't know what you want from me. I have to find a way home since you made me miss my ride."

"I'll take you home. Listen, I need you to help me. You're pretty good at raising money. I saw how quickly you helped the Honor Society get new shirts. I need some money."

"For what?"

"To fix my problem."

"Wait a minute. What do you mean by 'fix'?" "I can't keep this baby, Tawanda. Could you really see me raising a kid?"

"I couldn't see you raising a baboon, but that's not the point. You can't just kill your baby."

"You're not the one who's pregnant, Tawanda. You don't understand what I'm going through."

"Oh, I understand plenty. And you understand what you did to get the baby. Besides, your family has money, and I'm sure they'll help you take care of your child."

"Tawanda," she started, "we may live in the kind of house you could only dream of having, and we may have all the niceties that you scrape and struggle for all the time, but when it comes to family, I have to admit you have me beat. I really can't have this baby. Please help me."

After a long pause and an extremely long sigh, I finally said, "Ok, I'll help you. But on one condition."

"Anything."

"You have to keep the baby."

"I thought you were going to help me," she cried.

"I am. Now come on," I said while pulling her up. "We'll go to my house to think out our game plan."

Now my mama isn't one to like unannounced guests, but that's why she makes sure the house stays clean at all times. I figured she wouldn't mind if I brought Hannah. After all, I was trying to be nice and do something good for somebody.

"Hey, T-baby," Mama said when I walked in the door. I could already tell she wasn't so happy about our visitor when she asked, "Who's your friend?"

"I'm Hannah," she blurted before I could answer, "and we're not friends. Tawanda's helping me on a project."

Mama and I exchanged glances and rolled our eyes. "T, come into the kitchen for a minute. Make yourself at home, Hannah."

"What are you up to now?" Mama asked me. I explained Hannah's situation and told her how I was trying to be a Good Samaritan. "You don't know how to counsel anybody about babies."

"Well, you counsel her then. I couldn't think of anything else to say at the time, so I told her to come here and we would think of something together."

Mama didn't like me putting her in the middle of things, but she was sorta stuck this time. We went back into the living room where Hannah was looking a bit uncomfortable. I guess she wasn't used to sitting on second-hand furniture.

"Hannah," Mama began, "Tawanda explained your situation to me." Hannah shot me a glare that could have burned a hole in the wall. "Don't be mad at Tawanda. She's just trying to help."

"Well, I don't need any help," she replied. "I just need to go home now. I guess what my mother always says is true after all."

"What's that?"

"It's hard to find good help these days. I trusted you, Tawanda. I didn't tell you to go blabbing my business to your mother."

"Look, she can probably help your little whining hide. Besides, she understands what you're going through."

"Hannah," Mama said, "I was young when I had Marcus. You remember him?"

"No, I didn't know him, but Tawanda talks about him all too often," she replied.

Mama went on to tell her about all she went through with her folks to have Marcus. Then she talked about how Hannah would be better off having the baby. I was pretty bored with the whole thing 'cause I knew Hannah was going to do what she wanted to do anyway. She's all about herself – her hair, her nails, her boyfriends. She could never pull herself away from all that to take care of a baby. By the time she left, it was time for bed.

Today, I get to school and guess who's acting like we're best friends – Hannah, of course. I'm thinking, "What happened since yesterday?" So I asked her.

"Tawanda, I'm just so happy now. Your mom explained things so clearly."

"So, what did you decide to do?"

"I'm going to have the baby."

"What did she say that made you change your mind?"

"Well, she basically put it like this: 'If you don't have the baby, you'll spend the rest of your life wondering what he looks like and wondering if you could have been a better parent to him than your parents are to you.' So, I'm keeping it. Thanks, Tawanda."

"Don't thank me. Thank my mother."

"I did already. I might name it after her if it's a girl. What's your mom's first name?"

"Brenda."

"Ugh, that's not cute. Maybe some kind of derivation of 'Brenda' would work, like Brendalyn or something like that."

"Maybe." I was half listening to Hannah. Something still wasn't right. "What did your parents say about it?"

"Oh, I haven't told them and don't plan to," she said cheerfully. "They don't need to know. I don't think they'd really care one way or another. By the time the baby comes, I'll have moved in with Josh.

They won't even notice I'm gone." She was so nonchalant about the whole thing.

"I think your parents need to know," I said. "You can't hide their grandchild from them."

"I can and I will," she retorted.

I couldn't understand what was going on. Something about this just wasn't right. I couldn't put my finger on it, but Hannah was way too happy. Maybe she's just excited. Throughout my chorus class second block with Ms. O'Shea, Hannah plagued my mind. I was supposed to be singing an A flat note, but no sound was coming from my mouth. I didn't even notice the bell ring for the next class.

"Tawanda, are you okay?" It was Josh Ramsey. He was snapping his fingers in front of my face, which I never would have allowed under any other circumstances.

"Yeah," I said after I finally left my daze. "I don't know what's gotten into me."

"I think I know," he replied. "I know Hannah's been talking to you about this baby situation, but actually Tawanda, there is no baby."

"What do you mean 'no baby'? Hannah practically begged me to help her figure out some plan to help her get out of it. She didn't get rid of it, did she?"

"No. There never was a baby. She said that so you would talk to her."

"Wait a minute. I'm not following you."

"Hannah is going to run for Miss Homecoming this year. She figured she already had support from most of the students, but she thought that if she could create a friendship with the most feared girl in school, then she could secure the title."

I was not believing my ears. That little low-down-good-for-nothing-using-a-fake-pregnancy-to- get-a-friend-self. "Why are you telling me this?"

"Hannah wants to secure the votes from the athletes, too. I got wind of her little shenanigan and thought you should know."

"Well, how was she going to have a fake baby?" I asked.

"She was going to pretend that she had a miscarriage. That way, she would really get some sympathy from you as well as from the other students."

This was so low. I couldn't believe I'd been played by a little rich girl. I had to figure something out. I had to figure out a way to get her back for this. I wonder how long she anticipated on pretending she was pregnant? "I have a plan, Josh, and I need your help."

"Sure, whatever you say."

That night, I went home and read up on the Miss Homecoming rules and regulations. Obviously, Hannah had misunderstood the rules, which clearly stated that Miss Homecoming must not be the mother of any children or have been pregnant at any time as this reflects poor judgment on her part and could influence other students to do the same. I'm sure no one had thought to update these rules since 1953, but they worked for me today.

A few weeks later, it was time to vote for Miss Homecoming.

"How's the baby, Hannah?" I asked her at lunch one day.

"Oh, the baby's fine. The doctor said everything's good so far. Now remember, Tawanda, you can't tell anyone about this baby. I want to wait until the time is right."

"I understand completely," I responded.

At the Homecoming assembly at school, it is tradition for the girls' escorts to introduce them. I couldn't wait for Josh to introduce Hannah. I didn't know what he would say, but I knew it would be good.

"Last, we have Mr. Josh Ramsey introducing Miss Hannah Johnson," Mr. James announced.

"The person I am introducing today is a very good friend of mine. She is a member of the National Honor Society, Key Club, Latin Club, and Study Club.

She is president of the FBLA and is secretary of the Science Honor Society..."

Josh went on and on about Hannah's achievements. I was beginning to worry. Hannah wasn't. She was sitting there basking in her own glory. She just knew she was going to win this thing.

"... But most of all," Josh continued, "I want to thank her for choosing not to abort our child, which is due in June. For that, I am eternally grateful."

Everyone was gaping. Flies could have gone in and out of everybody's mouths a dozen times. Mr. James whispered something in Josh's ear, and Josh nodded and smiled.

"I'm sorry everyone," Mr. James started, "we must postpone the remainder of this assembly until we find out more information about this situation. Thank you. You are dismissed."

When I got home, I told my mother everything that had happened. She laughed but didn't think what Hannah did was funny. "I didn't think so either,

Mama." Suddenly, someone was banging on the back door.

"Now who could that be knocking on my door at this time of night? I hope they don't wake your sister. She's been ill all day," Mama said while peeping through the window. "Oh, it's your friend," she giggled while opening the door.

"Hi, Ms. Billups," Hannah said with downcast eyes.

"Hello, Hannah. Come on in. What are you doing out at this hour?"

"My parents put me out. They think I'm pregnant."

"Well, aren't you?" I asked just to see what she was gonna say.

"Tawanda, I'm sorry. I'm not pregnant. I only did that to get votes. I didn't think it would happen like this."

"Hannah," Mama said, "you don't need to pretend to be someone you're not just to get people to like you or vote for you. Just be yourself. If you can't do that, then it's not worth it in the first place."

"Why don't my parents ever talk to me like that? They're always talking about statistics and numbers, the Dow Jones, how much money they'll lose if you black people don't keep buying up everything, why everybody must get to know people with money because money makes more money. I really envy you, Tawanda."

"I'm going to pretend I didn't even hear that comment about us black people, but I must say, I do have it good," I smiled. Mama playfully jabbed me in the side. "I'm sure if we explain all this to your parents, they'll let you come back home."

"I'm not sure I want to go back. I like it here."

Mama had this look on her face, which I knew meant "No way, Jose."

"Hannah, whenever you need someone to talk to, I'm always here. But, baby, you can't stay here. You have a home. You have parents who love you.

They just show it in a different way. Now, come on, let's see if we can't get this straight with them."

Lesson learned: Being friendly is one thing; trusting people is another. I hope Hannah learned her lesson as did I.

Marcus

(1991)

Isn't it funny how you can remember everything about some days and nothing about others? Like I'm trying to remember what I wore to school last week so I won't do any repeats, but I can't remember a thing. I promised Mama I wouldn't write in detail about the real truth of Marcus's death, but I think at this point, I at least owe you that.

It was a Wednesday. The day before, Marcus and I had gone to the movies to see *Boyz 'N the Hood*. Of course, it was R rated, and neither of us was supposed to watch it. But Marcus and I did a lot of things we weren't supposed to do. Just like that time we went swimming in the pool at the Rec. Everybody was allowed to swim at the Rec, but Marcus and I went in November when the pool was closed. It wasn't as cold as some may like to think it was, but we were both sick for about two weeks after that.

When we got home, Mama had said, "Where you two been? Y'all're soakin' wet."

Marcus was always the one to come quick with a lie, so I held my peace in hopes that he could think of something quick. He didn't.

"I said 'Where you two been?'" Mama was hot now. She usually put one hand on her hip and held something else in her other hand like a spatula or a belt or whatever was near at the moment. This time, both hands were on her hips, which meant trouble.

"I—uh, we were down at the park and, uh," I looked to Marcus to help me out.

"Yeah, Mama," he started, "and June and July Jones was outside and they had they dog and they started messing with me and T so we started running and on the way we ran into Miss Nelia's sprinklers. T fell and that dog was almost on us, but we kept going."

"Yeah," I jumped in. "And we had to hide in some bushes so the dog wouldn't see us." Marcus gave me one of those we-were-already-home-free-why'd-you-have-to-add-your-two-cents looks. I gave him an I'm-sorry look.

"Just get in that house," Mama fumed.

We didn't get in trouble that day, but Mama and Daddy liked keeping us in suspense. Two weeks after the pool incident, we walked through the door laughing about May Jones falling in the cafeteria at Marcus's school. We didn't even get in the door good when Daddy came at us with his belt. A couple days after the whipping, I asked Daddy what the whipping was for.

"For lying two weeks ago about where y'all been. I know you was down there in that pool at the Rec and you know you didn't have no business being there."

Man, were they good.

But they didn't catch us this time about going to the movies. I guess in hindsight it was like God knew Marcus wouldn't be around for another whipping anyway, so why bother. I knew the guy who shot my brother very well. His name is Harold Pettigrew. Harold lived three blocks away from us on Tomlin Avenue. Even though we were only three blocks away, everybody knew to stay away from Tomlin Avenue. It was a hustler's hangout. Harold was two years older than Marcus, but they were in the same grade. Marcus liked the adventurous lifestyle Harold always talked about, so they became good friends. Harold would come over to our house and eat dinner with us many nights. His mother, Miss Louise, was a very hard-working woman. Every time I went to the post office to drop off a bill for Mama, Miss Louise would stop helping customers and shout "Hey T-baby!" so loud, I thought I would surely be deaf by the time I left the building. She worked two other jobs as well – janitor at the high school at night and bus driver for the city on weekends. I don't think I've ever seen her at her house, but I saw lots of Harold.

But, the few months before Marcus died, he and Harold stopped being so close. We saw less and less of Harold. At the post office one day, I asked Miss Louise where Harold had been since I hadn't seen much of him. She shouted, "OH, YOU KNOW HE BEEN

DOWN AT THE DETENTION CENTER. HE COME HOME IN THREE DAYS." I'm sure she didn't want that broadcast all over the post office, but I guess she couldn't help herself none.

I had told Marcus about it when I got home. He just shrugged it off and said he already knew. "So, what happened?"

"Nothing for you to worry about," he snapped.

I just went to my room after that and tried not to think about it. Marcus used to tell me everything. "Hey, T," he said coming into my room after a few minutes. "I know you want to know what's going on, but you're just too young to really understand all this."

I was utterly offended. "Too young? Since when, Marcus? I should know, too because if you're in trouble then I need to protect you."

He laughed. "*You* protect *me*? Let me worry about the protecting."

"So, are you gonna tell me or not 'cause if not I can find something else that little girls do like play with Barbie dolls." He knew I wasn't serious. I had never played with a doll in my life nor did I want to.

"Ok, it's like this. Me and Harold went down to Mr. Havisham's store a few months ago. You know what I went to get –"

"Yeah, garlic bologna," I giggled.

"You got it! Harold wanted some chips and cookies and some other junk. He was still looking around when I went to pay for my bologna. You know how Mr. Havisham is, so I was trying to hurry out the store 'cause I didn't have time to wash my hands and didn't want a repeat of the last time we went." I nodded that I knew what he meant.

He continued, "But Harold didn't come behind me. I turned back to see if he was coming and I caught him lifting his shirt to flash his gun at Mr. Havisham. Then, he walked out the store. I stood there stunned for all of thirty seconds when Harold told me to come on. T, I ain't never been that scared in my life."

"So, what happened? What did Mr. Havisham do?"

"I don't know what he did, but I told Harold I had to go home. You remember that day I came home sweating and Mama asked me if I was sick?"

"Oh, yeah, that's when you thought you had the flu or something and you didn't go to school for a week."

"The next day while you were at school and Mama and Daddy were gone to work, Mr. Havisham stopped by. He knew I was home 'cause Sid told him. He asked me who the young man was that I was with. He said he knew I was good and that I didn't have anything to do with it, but if I didn't tell him, he would have to tell the police that I was there, too."

So, Marcus told. After that, Harold didn't trust him and couldn't stand to see him. I felt bad for Marcus 'cause that was his friend. When Harold got out of the detention center, he was mad at the world. I don't know what happened to him in there, but he was not happy. He used to go shopping for his mama, but she said he wouldn't do anything but hang out with the bad kids on his street.

On this particular Wednesday, it was so hot outside I could fry a slice of fat back on the pavement. Marcus and I ate the pancakes, Concecuh sausage, and scrambled eggs that Daddy cooked before he left for work. Mama had told me to walk Shanice down to the babysitter Mrs. Henson.

"T-baby, let's go 'round to the Rec today. I'ma teach you how to play speed." I beamed to hear Marcus say that. I had been wanting to learn this card game for some time now. All the folks knew how to play at my school was Uno, so I would be the first kid with such knowledge.

"Ok, but I gotta run Shanice down to Mrs. Henson's first."

"I'll go with you. Then we can shoot over to the Rec."

We set out with Shanice in Marcus's arms and walked the two blocks to Mrs. Henson's. Her house reminded me of a bread store. She always had something baking in the oven, and she sometimes gave us a piece of cake or pie if we were good.

The recreation center was just four more blocks away. "Tawanda, you ever get a weird feeling?" Marcus asked as I slowly sipped the cool water Mrs. Henson gave me.

"Yeah, in my stomach sometimes, but it's just gas. If you about to blow one, let me know *please*."

"Naw, not like that, T. I mean like something's gonna happen – good or bad."

"No, I don't think so. Why? You think something's gonna happen?"

"Well, I don't know. I just been feeling like that for a few days." He shrugged his shoulders and we continued our walk.

I saw Harold first. He had his Kool Moe Dee shades on and jeans down to what seemed like his ankles. "Yo, Marcus!" he yelled. Marcus turned to see Harold standing across the street pointing a gun straight at him. Then, he pushed me so hard I fell off the sidewalk onto the street just as Harold's gun went off. When I looked up, Harold and about three other guys stood staring before they ran up the street and darted down an alley. I crawled over to where Marcus had fallen. He was screaming.

"Marcus!" I screamed as I beat his chest. "Marcus!" I cried. I could hardly see him for the fountain of tears. "Marcus!"

"T-baby," he struggled. "Ahhh! Ahhh! It hurts so bad, T."

"Hang on, Marcus. Let me get some help." I looked up from Marcus to see a couple of people coming out of their houses. "Help!" I yelled. "Help! Help me! Help my brother!" I was bawling. My tears blurred my vision as I looked back at Marcus who had stopped crying.

He struggled to speak, "Do...me...a ... fav...always 'member you ... beautiful ... you can do whatever you want."

"No, Marcus! That's what people say in movies when they dying. You not dying!"

"I love you. Tell Mama…" he gulped for air, "I love her, and Daddy and Shanice and Grandma…" His voice trailed off. He was gone.

I lay there next to my brother for a long time. I didn't want to leave him. The ambulance came and took him away from me – forever.

Uncle June

2001

I've always been one to believe that what goes around, comes back to kick you in the butt. I also believe that when you grow up poor, the first one to make it out should be the first one to come back and bring everybody else out. But despite my latter belief, there are some folks you just can't get through to. Take my Uncle June Bug for example. Oh, excuse me; it's Darryl Jonathan Billups, Jr., my daddy's brother.

When we were living in Jersey, everybody was broke and struggling. Nobody tried to out-do anybody,\ and all the neighbors were nice and let you have a cup of sugar when you didn't have any. Uncle June Bug, which he didn't mind anybody calling him then, would come over every Sunday and eat dinner with us. Mama didn't mind 'cause Uncle June would return the favor by cutting our grass that evening. That's how he made his money. He would cut anybody's grass at any time of the day. One summer, he even had a heat stroke cutting Euclid Harris's grass. Daddy had told him not to do it.

"June, you bet not go cut no yard in this heat," Daddy had told him.

"Man, you know if I don't cut no grass, I don't eat. Besides, Mr. Harris got a lotta yard, so I know he gonna pay me good."

"Well, don't come cryin' to me when you fall out with a stroke." That was it. Uncle June was jinxed. He only had a light set back. The next week, he was up cutting grass again. Euclid Harris had the nerve to get mad 'cause only half his grass was cut. So Daddy went and finished the job and gave Uncle June the money. Daddy could be nice like that sometimes.

I remember Uncle June telling Marcus one time that he was going to own his very own landscaping business one day and make six figures. I didn't know what the six figures were then, but I was pretty sure it had to be good for him to brag about it like he did. Marcus told him he'd work for him, but of course he never got the chance. Right after Marcus died, Uncle June finally got his wish. He opened up Marcus Landscaping Company and started making pretty good money.

Right before we moved to Alabama, he told Mama, "Now, Brenda, just because you and my brother ain't married no more, you still Sis to me. I won't forget you when I make them big bucks." Apparently, he got a slight case of amnesia 'cause we've been in Alabama for five years, and we hadn't heard a peep from Uncle June until yesterday.

He comes driving up in his shiny black Hummer, which I'm sure he had to fill up at least thirteen times on his way down here, which of course I think is a waste of good money that could be sitting in my savings account for college.

"Hey, T-baby," he said when I answered the door. "You so big now. What grade you in?" He smiled, and I was surprised to see he still had that one gold tooth in front that he swore he would remove when he "made it big." Some things, I guess, never change.

"Twelfth grade," I said as I ushered him in.

"Where ya Mama at?" He looked around as if he didn't know if he should sit down, so he just stood there.

"She's at work, Uncle June," I said, "but you can have a seat. She'll be here in about thirty minutes." I looked at my watch. "Elgin should be here any minute."

"Who's Elgin?"

"You didn't know my mama got remarried? His name is Elgin Howard Lewis the Third."

"What a name. Naw, I didn't know. I bet your daddy don't know neither. You know he got him a little friend. He say he ain't thinking about marrying nobody though. I think he know he missed out on a good thang wit ya mama."

"Yeah, well, that saga is over, Uncle June."

"Okay, baby. And you know I don't go by June Bug no more. It's Uncle Darryl." He grinned again;

109

and looking at that gold tooth, I thought, "Yeah, right."

"So, what y'all been up to? Where that Shanice at? I know she 'bout grown now."

"She's eleven and at a friend's house right now. What about you? You got any kids?"

He grinned that little sheepish schoolboy grin and started twiddling his fingers.

"That's part of my surprise," he gleamed. "They're out in the truck – my wife and daughter, that is."

"Well, why didn't you bring them in?" I threw my hands up, rolled my eyes, and headed outside toward the chrome-detailed Hummer. Uncle June is too old for this kind of stuff, I thought.

"T-baby, hold up," Uncle June said, catching up to me. I was half-way down the walkway and wondered what the wife and kid thought about being made to sit in the truck while Uncle June had been in the house all that time. "Hold up, girlie. There's something you should—"

"Uncle Darryl, you should be ashamed of yourself, leaving your family out here in the sun. Let 'em come in the house." I proceeded to the truck and opened the front passenger door. Before the woman inside could get out a good "Hello," I slammed the door and looked at my reflection in the tinted window.

"T-baby, I was trying to explain before you did that. Bethany is white."

"Duh, I think that's quite obvious now isn't it?"

"What you got against white people anyway, T? She human just lak you."

"I don't have anything against white people, Uncle June. I just can't believe you married one. You, who used to always talk about 'the white man be tryin' to hold me down, T. I can't get a break except to break my neck.' What did my daddy say?"

"Ya daddy don't have nothing to do with this, but he met her. It took some gettin' used to, but he okay wit it. Look, we been married four years, and our

111

little girl Makayla is three. You'll love her, T. She the cutest thang."

I guess people do change. I distinctly remember Uncle June telling me never to bring home a white man, never to let white people be my friends, never to tell a white person any details about my life. Now, this man who ingrained these thoughts into my mind has gone against his very own words. The least he could do is acknowledge he was wrong. But, I decided I would just leave that alone. Besides, I haven't seen or heard from him in forever, and it'll probably be another forever before I see him again. I could tolerate him for a few –

"How long are you planning to be in town, Uncle June – I mean, Darryl?"

"I don't know. A few days maybe. Can we please open the door now, and apologize to Bethany, will ya?"

"Fine," I muttered as I opened the door. She didn't look too bad. She was obviously much younger than my uncle. I'm sure she's closer to my age than his, and she could stand to work on her makeup a bit. I immediately noticed her Dolly Parton chest, which I'm sure was the first thing June noticed as well. At least it wasn't hanging out like some folks have theirs. Her turquoise shrug and matching pedal pushers outfit was cute.

"Hi," I said. "Sorry I slammed the door in your face."

"That's okay, hun," she responded popping what smelled like Big Red. "I get that all the time." She hopped out and went to the back to let her daughter out. Makayla was the cutest kid I'd seen in a long time. She reminded me of Olivia on *The Cosby Show.*

"Say 'Hi,' Makayla," Bethany said.

"Hi." Makayla even sounded like Olivia. She reached out to shake my hand, so I did.

"K-K, this is your cousin Tawanda. But we all call her T-baby." That was Uncle June.

He was grinning from ear to nose (He had a crooked smile ever since that heat stroke back in the day). "Ain't she smart, T?"

I couldn't really tell from "Hi," but I said "She sure is" just to make him feel good. "Well, let's go inside. It's hot out here." I wondered what Mama would think when she got home. She's not too fond of strange people being in her house without her knowing. Like that time I brought Hannah Johnson and her lying self home to help her. I tell you, you just can't trust folks these days.

Anyway, Makayla and Uncle June and Bethany had made themselves at home on the couch when Mama pulled up. I kind of liked Bethany. She wasn't like Mrs. Sarah Jane Jackson who married the deacon at our church and thought she had to start "acting black" in order to belong. She was just being herself, which I rather like.

"Hey, T-baby," Mama yelled from the back door. "Whose Hummer is that outside? Did they get lost or something? And you know better than to 'low folks in the house 'specially when I ain't home…" I could hear Mama struggling with what sounded like grocery bags, so I ran to help her.

"No, Mama, I don't think they're lost. It's Uncle June."

"June?" Before I could get another word out, Mama was flying into the living room to see her former brother-in-law. "Hey, June! Get up from there and give me a hug, man. How you doing?"

"Oh, I'm fine. How you—"

"June, who is this?" Mama was trying to be as polite as she could, but I knew she wasn't pleased to see Bethany sitting there.

"Oh, this is my wife, Bethany. Bethany, this is my sis-in-law, Brenda."

"Nice to meet ya, hun," Bethany said popping her gum. She reached out to hug my mama, but Mama pulled back.

"June, you didn't tell us you got married. How long ago has this been?"

"Oh, uh, four years. And, Brenda, just call me Darryl. I don't go by June no more."

"Oh, I see. You done left your roots. You went and made it big and to show us all you made it big, you went and married her."

"Naw, that ain't how it is."

"Darryl, I don't need anybody taking up for me," Bethany chimed in. "I can tell when I'm not wanted. Makayla and I will go sit in the truck and wait for you. Take your time." Bethany was obviously upset. Black people have been known to be the most accepting people in the world. But, that's before you meet my mama. I wonder what her family thinks of Uncle June.

"Now, why'd you have to go and get her all upset, Brenda? She's my wife, and I love her. It don't have nothing to do with color."

"I'm sure it don't, June, Darryl, whatever the hell your name is. I got dinner to cook. Elgin'll be home in a minute, and I need to get started on it.

What brings you here anyway? You must want something."

"Well, I came to make good on my word. You know, your word is your bond as they say. So, now that I done made it big, I came to give you your just due."

"My, my, my. I didn't think you'd do it, June. But, really, you don't have to do anything for us. We're pretty self-sufficient around here."

I had to chime in then. I knew my mama was not going to let Uncle June walk out of here without giving us something. "Uh, Mama, let's hear what the man has to say."

"Thank you, T. Now, I want to give all the kids some money in they accounts for college. Fifty thousand each for T and Shanice. And another fifty thousand for you."

Mama's eyes grew big and round. "No, June, I can't take that money. You can give the kids what you want, but don't worry about me. It just wouldn't be right."

"Hellooo, I'm home," Elgin called from the back door. "Whose Hummer is that outside?" He walked into the room and saw Uncle June and immediately looked at Mama for an explanation.

"Hey, Elgin, this is my Uncle Darryl, my daddy's brother. He came from New Jersey to give us some money," I crooned.

"Oh, hey, well as long as there's money involved, you're most welcomed." Elgin laughed and shook Uncle June's hand.

"Yeah, I was just telling Brenda that I was giving her fifty thousand dollars, but she don't want it."

Elgin looked at Mama like she had a third eye. "Baby, what's the matter? Take the money."

"Look at it this way," Uncle June started. "It's the part Marcus would've gotten."

I stopped fidgeting with my hair and looked at Mama. It seemed as though tears were forming at the corners of her eyes. Nobody had mentioned Marcus in a few months. Even though it had been almost ten years since he died, we all get a bit jumpy at the sound of his name sometimes.

Mama started slowly, "Yeah, I guess you're right, huh?" She wiped her hands on her pants and started toward the kitchen. "Darryl, make yourself at home, hear?"

I wondered what Mama was thinking. Sometimes I could read her face, sometimes I couldn't. It just depended on the situation. I thought Mama should really consider taking Uncle June's money. After all, he did promise it to her all those years ago. And, like I always say, you have to give back to those who gave to you.

"Brenda," Uncle June started, "I'm sorry if I've upset you. You know I wouldn't just use Marcus's name for no reason. But look, Sis, this money belongs to Marcus. Hell, the company is named after him. He should get something, and I don't see no better way of giving him his just due than by giving his mama his share."

Mama left for the kitchen and busied herself with flour and chicken. She was definitely bothered. Whenever she was upset about something, she cooked chicken. One time Marcus was late coming home from school. I was in preschool and had gotten home early. Marcus was apparently supposed to be home by the time we got back from the store. Mama called several parents, but no one had seen him. Then, she started cooking chicken. She was slapping wings and legs around in a bowl of flour and literally throwing them over into the pan of hot, popping grease. Marcus eventually showed up and explained that he had been at the park with some friends and lost track of time. Needless to say, Mama didn't care what his excuse was. He got a real whipping and never came home late again.

Now, Mama was doing the same thing with the chicken, but she stopped long enough to come back into the living room to answer Uncle June. "June, I guess you're right," Mama began. "I just feel a little guilty about taking what is supposed to be his. But, he's not here, and we can't undo what's been done. We've been through all that already. Can we maybe start some kind of organization for parents who've lost children or something like that?"

Uncle June beamed. "Sis, you can do whatever you want with it. That organization thing sounds real good. I'm sure there're a lot more parents out there like you who need some help."

Mama hugged Uncle June and thanked him. Meanwhile, there still remained the matter of Bethany and Makayla. Uncle June had not forgotten. "Now," he stated with an air of finality, "what we gonna do about my wife? We was gonna stay here a couple of days and visit with y'all, but seeing as she's white, I guess we'll haveta stay in a motel."

"Naw you don't, June," Mama smiled. She seemed to have made up her mind on Bethany.
"Yes, I would have preferred you to marry in your own race, since you used to preach about it so much, but so many of y'all aren't doing that these days, I guess you ain't no exception. I've always taught my kids to

121

love everybody, so I really shouldn't be like that. She can come on in. I'll treat her right, June."

"Thank you, Sis. And remember it's Darryl, not June no more."

"June, you can get out of my house with that Darryl mess. I know yo name is Darryl, but I call you June and I'ma keep calling you June till you ain't June no more. Now go on and get the girl out the car 'fore I change my mind."

Graduation

2001

Yesterday, at my high school graduation, I received the surprise of my life when my sixth grade English teacher Miss Vantage was introduced as the keynote speaker. At first, I didn't even know who she was. All I knew was that some nobody named Dr. Angela Turnbaum would be lecturing us on how to have a good life. Why couldn't we get Bill Cosby or Oprah or even Katie Couric? At least people know who *they* are. But when this Dr. Turnbaum (Really, who wouldn't have their name changed?) began to talk, I knew then that she was my old familiar friend Miss Vantage.

"Today marks a new day for all of you," she began. She no longer wore the granny glasses and the pink sweater she kept for those chilly mornings. She was actually quite beautiful, and I thought "What made her so lovely?"

"...Tawanda." I perked up then. "She was in my sixth grade English class when she and her family

123

lived in Newark, New Jersey. I knew one day she would be successful, and as your valedictorian, she is. Tawanda, I recall telling you that your brother Marcus had written his best essay about you, and I'm going to read a piece from it today."

I couldn't believe it. Miss Vantage was here, and she was going to give me Marcus's essay. I remember sitting in her ice box room that last day in her class staring out the single square window looking at nothing but the sagging leaves of the weeping willow tree outside. Miss Vantage had made me upset that day, but after my presentation, she told me about Marcus's essay. I wanted it then, but she said she didn't know where it was. For years, I had wondered just what Marcus had said about me. He had never mentioned it, and I was curious.

"... will read an excerpt. This is not only for Tawanda, but for all of you... 'My little sister Tawanda is my semi-precious jewel. I don't think older brothers and sisters understand just how important little sisters are. If they did, the world would be a better place.

Tawanda gives me what no one else can – unconditional love. No matter what I do, Tawanda is always there by my side. We do everything together – eat fried chicken, go fishing with Daddy, and dash in the waves at the beach. Most importantly, we encourage each other. When I was afraid Mama was going to spank me for playing a prank on Mr. McCorvey, it was Tawanda who told me it would be better to fess up to it. When Tawanda was upset because somebody called her round, I told her to just laugh at people like that, and she did.

"Daddy tells me sometimes that I should do more manly things than playing with my little sister all the time, but I believe you have to be yourself. If you can't do that, then what can you do? Being with Tawanda is what I do.'"

Miss Vantage – sorry, Dr. Turnbaum – paused for a moment. I could see tears streaming down her face smearing her mascara along the way. I could taste my own salty tears as they flowed uncontrollably. I couldn't see Mama, but I knew she must be crying, too.

She continued, "I only hope that one day I can be to Tawanda all that she has been to me. I love her. No matter what happens to me, I need for her to know that she is beautiful. I need her to know that loving me is the greatest gift she can give me. When she graduates high school, I'm going to give her this essay as her gift so she will know just how much I love her and how much she means to me.'" I could only see a blur of Miss Vantage through my tears. Marcus truly was my best friend.

"Marcus," she continued, "wrote this essay when he was in my sixth grade English class, four years before I taught Tawanda. Little did he know that he would not be with us today. One year after writing this essay, Marcus was senselessly gunned down in the middle of the day with his little sister right by his side as always. For no reason. So, I say to all of you today, show love now. Say 'I love you' now. You are graduating high school today. Marcus and so many others didn't get this opportunity. You are blessed, but don't stop here. You can become whatever you put your mind to, but none of that matters if you don't show love." I couldn't contain myself anymore. I ran over to Miss Vantage and gave her a huge hug. We cried together for what seemed like days before the principal Mr. Hurley came over to the microphone and said, "Congratulations, class of 2001!"

After the ceremony, we all went to eat at my favorite restaurant, including Dr. Turnbaum and her husband. Daddy even came after an awkward moment in the auditorium lobby. "You sure you don't mind me coming to dinner?" he asked to which I replied, "You're my daddy and I love you. Of course you can come to dinner. That is if it's okay with Mama." Mama smiled and agreed. It was like we were one big happy family again. We shared some good memories, but something was different. Sitting there at the table with all these people who loved me and who had loved Marcus, I discovered that I had

127

missed out so much on loving those who are still here. I do love Mama and Shanice and Daddy and Elgin and my new little brother Davis, but I wasn't giving them what I had given Marcus.

2007

As I look back over "A Situation that Caused Me to Change" and the other stories you've read in this book, I know I've grown a lot. Now, I can finally let Marcus rest in peace.

No, I'll never forget him, but I can move on now, knowing that I made his life a beautiful place to live in.

> Unconditional love
> is what they say
> You get when you're
> in love...
> I say
> it's what you give
> when your heart is
> saturated with peace.
> Thank you, Marcus,
> for Peace.
>
> -- Tawanda Michelle Billups

Epilogue

Brenda Maureen Davis Billups Lewis

Tawanda told me I needed to write something for this book, but I told her I didn't know the first thing about writing. We fussed about it for a whole week before I finally gave in and decided to sit down and write this thing.

I guess I should start when Marcus was born. Martin and I were high school sweethearts, and we just knew we'd be together forever. When I found out I was pregnant with Marcus, I was devastated. I was in the twelfth grade, and I had so many dreams of doing so many things. I was going to be a professional athlete – maybe basketball or softball. I was good at both. But when Marcus was born, those other things didn't matter any more. Marcus became my life, and Martin and I got married the next year and moved to New Jersey. Marcus brought us so much joy. He ran before he walked. One day Martin was teasing him, and Marcus started running around the dining room table to get away, laughing and drooling at the same time. He was something else.

He always tried to invent new things to do like the "Monster Machine." The Monster Machine was Marcus's re-enactment of the Incredible Hulk. Whenever his imaginary friends made him mad, he turned into the Monster Machine and tore them to shreds. It was hilarious to watch. I wish we had a video camera back then. He asked us one day if he could have a brother or a sister to play Monster Machine with. Martin and I just looked at each other. We hadn't given much thought to having more children before Marcus said that. After some consideration, we decided it would be good to have another baby.

Marcus was the happiest little fellow when we told him I was pregnant. Of course he had lots of questions about where babies came from, and I left Martin to that task. I still don't know exactly what Martin said to explain it, but Marcus never asked any questions about it again. He was four years old when

Tawanda was born. I don't think she knows this, but the doctors didn't think she would make it into this world. While I was in the delivery room, Tawanda's heart rate dropped a great deal.

For a moment they thought she had died, but I prayed harder than I've ever prayed in my life. Marcus was outside in the waiting room with my friend Shana. He told her to send me a message saying that he had prayed for God to save his little brother or sister and that he believed God heard him. I know he did because right after Shana left the room Tawanda's heart rate improved, and she was born a few minutes later. Marcus was allowed to come in the room soon after, and he wanted to name her immediately. I remember him climbing up on the hospital bed saying, "Let me name her, Mama. Let me name her, Daddy." Martin and I had already given thought to names. If we had a boy, his name would be Bernard Calvin. The girl name we had decided on was Michelle Alicia. Marcus had said, "That's not a good name for a girl." So we asked him what he thought her name should be. "Let me see," he pondered for a while with his finger to his chin as if he were in deep thought. "I know – Tawanda!" He said it was a pretty name, so we decided to name her that and give our name, Michelle, as her middle name.

Marcus insisted that he also get to choose her nickname, and that's why we call her T-baby.

From day one those two were inseparable. They spent every minute they could together. They thought I didn't know about all those adventures they had – especially the fire at Aunt Cicily's Chicken Shack. I even knew about the seemingly crafty cover-up of Mr. Havisham's flood. I tried to interrogate them one-on-one, but those two stuck together no matter what. Martin would have fits sometimes because he couldn't depend on either one of them to tell the truth about what the other one had done. Neither one of them could imagine being without the other for any length of time.

When Shanice was born, they pretty much ignored her at first. She threw a loop in their plans.

She couldn't go everywhere they went, so they would get mad if I told them to stay home and play with their little sister. By the time Shanice learned to walk, they were taking her with them, too. She became one of the gang.

Then Marcus was killed.

My baby was taken away from me, and I wasn't there to do anything about it. To add to the pain, Tawanda was there with him as usual when it happened, and she held him until he died. Coping with a traumatized daughter after a son has been murdered has to be one of the most difficult things to do. But we made it. Even though Martin and I divorced, we've mended our differences and have moved on with our lives.

I've watched Tawanda mature into a beautiful young woman. Her writing proves that. I was really worried for her right after Marcus died – he was her world. But, Tawanda still shines as one of those individuals who can stare Adversity in the face and tell it off. She has no problem speaking her mind. Her greatest asset can sometimes be her greatest drawback, too.

I was hesitant to read this book because I didn't know what she might say about me. But, I don't care about that now. Tawanda does a great service to all the young people in the world who have lost a sibling to violence. It really is an epidemic in Black America. It is an epidemic that must be stopped.

Every time I turn on the television, another young boy or girl has been senselessly gunned down or stabbed or raped or maimed. What many people fail to realize is that the person who commits the crime is not just taking away the life of the person they've killed. They're also taking away the joy that others like Tawanda have. Harold took peace away from my baby. But thank God she got it back. Others like Tawanda can learn how to take back their joy and peace that the devil stole from them. For those who want to know, Harold is serving a life sentence with no possibility of parole. His friends, his accomplices, are serving 40-year sentences. I don't take any joy in that. They were the same age as Marcus. Their mothers, sisters, and brothers are grieving their losses just like we grieve ours.

In the end, no one wins. But we can learn to love again. And, we can empower others to do the same.

www.ingramcontent.com/pod-product-compliance
Lightning Source LLC
Chambersburg PA
CBHW051305250626
47155CB00009B/3447